To my daughter Sophie, my muse and best critic,
without whom Narda would never have been created.

Hi!

My name is Narda. I'm ~~eleven and a~~ almost twelve half years old.
I live in a really cool hotel in the Bahamas Islands
called Atlantis. It's always warm and sunny here.
You can swim all year long and there are plenty of
things to do.

I live with my dad except when he's away on
business, which is a lot. When he's not here Ms.
Colby comes to take care of things and
tutor me in English and stuff like History and
Math. She's really nice, but she has a lot of rules.

One day I want to be a writer so I'm writing
this story about all the things you can do here.

I hope you enjoy reading it.

Narda

Narda woke to reflections from the lagoon
below dancing on her ceiling. She was still
half-dreaming her favorite dream about Lost
Atlantis when Ms. Colby came in.
Narda wondered what plans she had for this
sunny day.

As they walked, Ms. Colby read from a thick book. "Remember, Narda," she said, "the most important thing in life is to always keep your mind open to new experiences."

They stopped at the House of Parliament. Ms. Colby read about it. Then she took pictures of it

Next they went to the Botanical Gardens. Ms. Colby read about the plants. Then she took pictures of them.

They went to the Straw Market. Ms. Colby read about crafts. Then she took pictures of baskets while Narda tried on hats.

After lunch, Ms. Colby asked Narda if there was anything else she wanted to see.

Narda said, "I would love to go to the beach. It's such a pretty day."

Ms. Colby sighed. She didn't care much for the beach, but after all, it was a pretty day.

Ms. Colby did her "don'ts" . . .

and Narda did her "won'ts ".

Don't go in too far

I won't

Don't stay in too long

I won't

Don't go into big waves

I won't

Ms. Colby took out her book and Narda ran happily into the ocean.

But she must have been swimming a long time, because when she came back Ms. Colby was fast asleep. The sun had shifted and Ms. Colby was already toasted to a bright pink.

The next morning Narda woke early. She knocked on Ms. Colby's door to find out what the day's plans were.

When she walked in, Ms. Colby was sitting up in bed, looking into a mirror and saying "Oh, my, oh my, oh my!" over and over again. Poor Ms. Colby! She was so sunburned she looked like a radish!

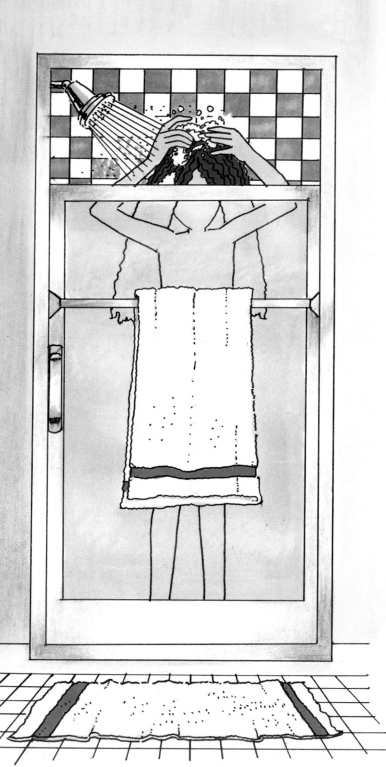

Narda jumped in the shower and washed her hair while cheerfully singing the Sponge Bob song off key.

She brushed her teeth with special attention to her braces just as Dr. Goldman had shown her.

She gazed lovingly at her sleek, perfectly straight wet hair . . .

then put on a Grinch face as it dried into its usual uncontrollably curly self.

She carefully selected clothing to wear . . .

and Ta Da! she was finally ready to join the free world.

With her stomach nicely contented, she walked down the main hall . . .

which always reminded her of the beautiful palace of her dreams . . .

and came to her favorite spot– the Throne of Atlantis– where she
often sat and imagined herself as the Princess of the Lost Continent.

The Dig was another of her favorites. It was the most incredible place! Like something in an Indiana Jones movie. There were huge windows where you could see weird old temples and statues, all underwater, with amazing fish swimming around them. It was right there that Narda got the idea to write her own story about Lost Atlantis.

The Story of
LOST ATLANTIS
by
Narda

A long, long, time ago there was a beautiful city called Atlantis. It was a wonderful place where everyone was happy because there was plenty of food and nice houses for people to live in. There were a lot of tall buildings with statues all around and parks where children could play and grownups could sit and read or take walks.

There were lots of nice trees and flowers and birds and a lot of butterflies. And there was no pollution. Atlantis was on the edge of the ocean. People had boats and caught fish and you could always go swimming there. The King of Atlantis was a very nice man but he had a lot to do and so he was always busy. He had a daughter who was a princess. Her name was Nardalina. She was almost 12 years old and she lived in a beautiful palace.

She loved to go to the beach and swim. One day Nardalina saw that the water was coming up higher on the beach every day. When it kept happening, she ran to her father to tell him. Only he was so busy he really didn't hear everything she said and he told her not to worry. But Nardalina kept seeing the water get higher and higher each day.

One day the fishermen came to her and said they were very worried because they never had seen the ocean get so high and they asked her to tell her father that there was danger, but he was away on business. Finally the ocean got so high that the waves were covering the streets and going into people's houses and all of the people were afraid. When the King did come back it was too late. The city and all the people disappeared under the sea and no one could ever find them and that's why they call it the City of Lost Atlantis.

Narda had a special spot in The Dig - a big round window where she liked to sit and listen to her music while she watched the fish glide past. Suddenly a huge shark stopped at her window and stared straight at her. She noticed that the shark was moving its head from side to side in time with her music.

Narda hopped up and began to move with him. Soon they were dancing together down the hall in perfect rhythm until finally Narda's battery ran down and they had to stop. Narda waved goodbye. The shark smiled, waggled his tail and glided away down the aquarium.

Ms. Colby still wasn't feeling well, so Narda headed off to the beach, where there was a tent where Bahamian ladies had set up shop. They sold all kinds of trinkets and clothing and you could even get your hair done in corn rows. Narda shuddered at the thought of anyone trying that on <u>her</u> hair.

She did find a bracelet that she liked and while she was trying it on Narda noticed people parasailing. "Parasailing!" thought Narda, "What a cool idea! " But what about Ms. Colby.? "Well, she didn't actually say I couldn't go, now did she?"

Minutes later she was flying high above the Caribbean under a silky, yellow and orange canopy, looking down at the toy buildings and tiny ant people on the island below. TOTALLY FANTASTIC!

Narda was back on the beach again when a girl about her age approached and said, "Hallo. My name is Marianne. May I sit with you?" She was French. She was wearing a bikini. And she had perfectly straight, shiny blonde hair that Narda would have died for.

In no time they were talking and laughing and Narda felt as though she had known Marianne forever.

The two girls swam and dove and surfed and chatted endlessly. Marianne's father was also a businessman who traveled a great de

When the coconut man came along they both had coladas.

Marianne said, "You have the most *formidable* hair I have ever seen! How I wish mine were like yours!" Narda said, "What? I've always wanted hair like yours!" She had never thought of her hair as *formidable* before, whatever that meant.

"Don't you get lonely when he goes away?" Narda asked. "Oh, no,"said Marianne, I go with him whenever I can."

"How do you do that?" asked Narda. Marianne replied, "Come with me for lunch and I'll show you."

The two walked to the marina. "This is how", said Marianne, pointing to the most humongous boat Narda had ever seen. "This is our floating home." The boat had eight bedrooms, a living room big enough for a major party, a dining room with 24 chairs, a den with a giant television, a gym, a swimming pool and much more.

Lunch was served at a table on an open deck. Narda didn't know the names for everything she ate but it was all delicious. "Can we meet again tomorrow?" Narda asked. "I wish we could," said Marianne sadly, "but we are leaving tonight. We must write each other." The girls exchanged e-mail addresses.

"You are my dear friend," Marianne said.

ie kissed Narda on both cheeks. "This is how we say goodbye in France."

Narda said, " I want you to keep my bag so you'll remember me."

And I want you to have mine, " said Marianne. "These bags will miss their owners,

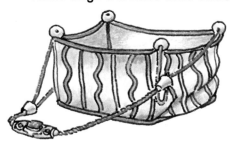

so we must be sure that they meet again."

On the way back, Narda let her hair go free. It felt *formidable*. And she suddenly felt pretty in a way she never had before.

Ms Colby was feeling better but she still wasn't ready to go out . She apologized for leaving Narda alone for so long. "I'm fine," Narda said. "Really. I've found things to keep me busy."

She was glad Ms. Colby didn't ask her what kinds of things!

The next morning Narda tried out the water slides, first ,the small ones, then the double slide, then the twisty one that went around in circles in the dark, where she screamed happily with all the other kids .

but played it very cool and mature at the end.

That afternoon she found something even more exciting. She went out snorkeling on a nearby reef and discovered a whole world of fish of every shape and size. They were incredible! She decided she wanted to make a painting of them.

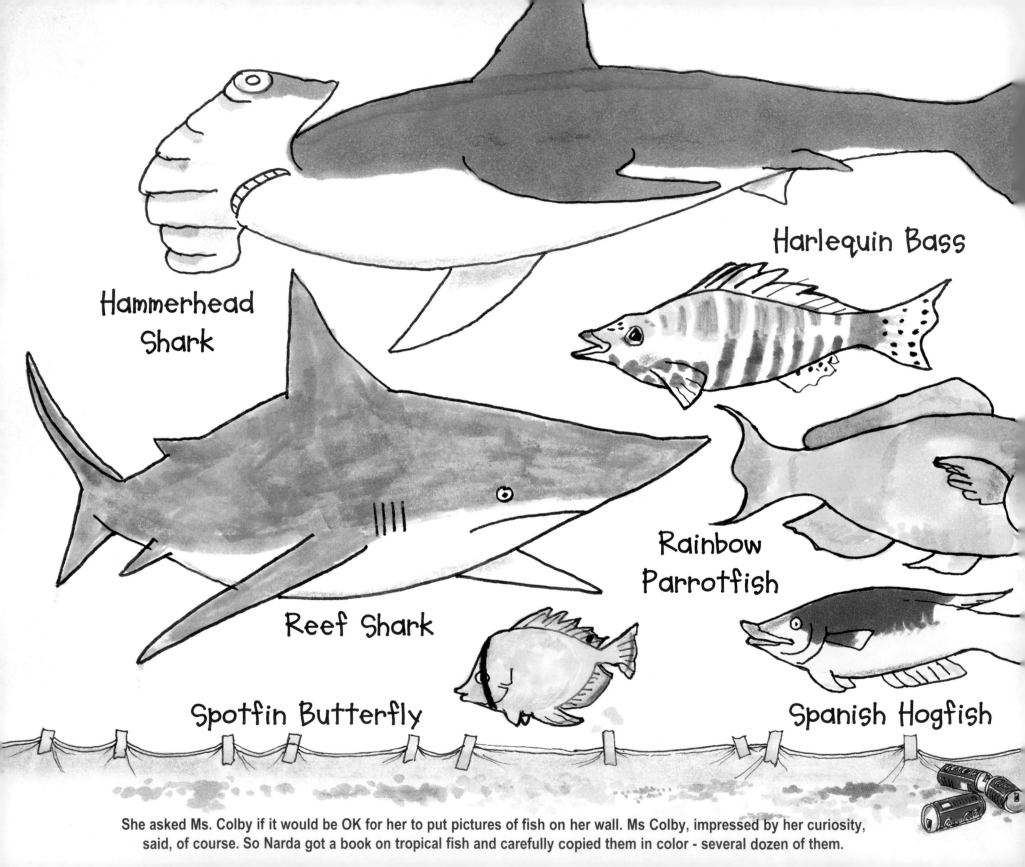

Harlequin Bass

Hammerhead
Shark

Reef Shark

Rainbow
Parrotfish

Spotfin Butterfly

Spanish Hogfish

She asked Ms. Colby if it would be OK for her to put pictures of fish on her wall. Ms Colby, impressed by her curiosity, said, of course. So Narda got a book on tropical fish and carefully copied them in color - several dozen of them.

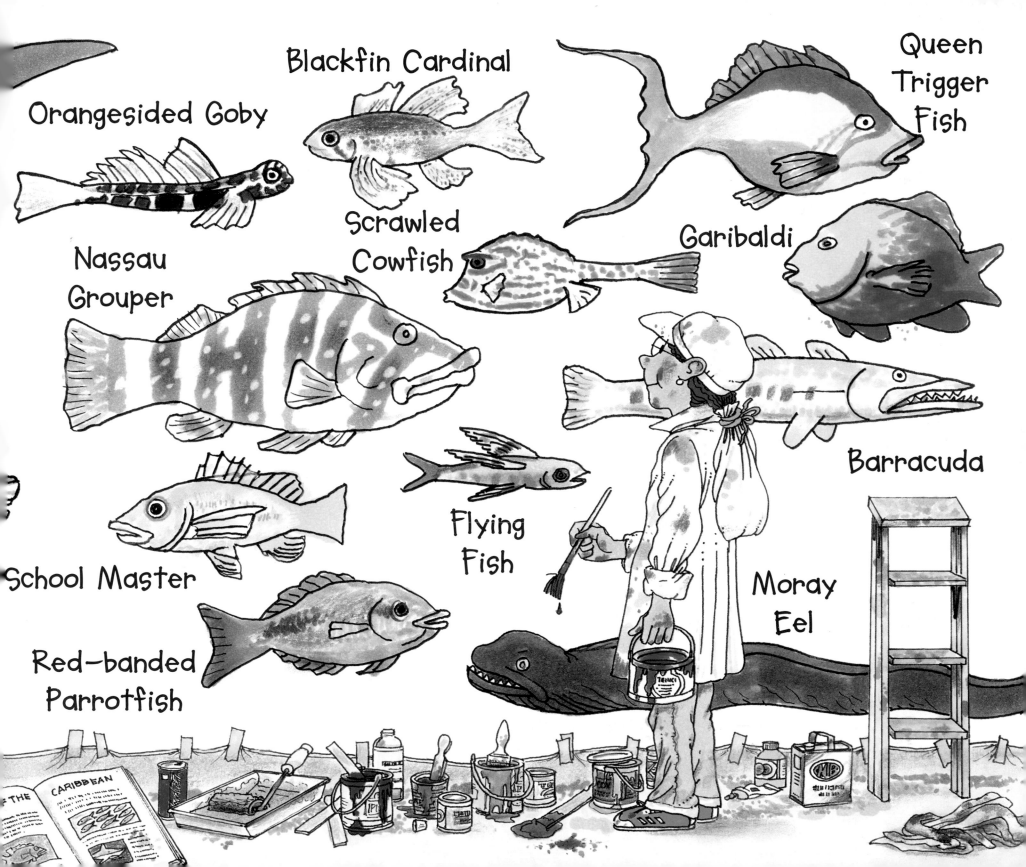

Orangesided Goby

Blackfin Cardinal

Queen Trigger Fish

Scrawled Cowfish

Garibaldi

Nassau Grouper

Barracuda

Flying Fish

School Master

Moray Eel

Red-banded Parrotfish

CARIBBEAN

Ms. Colby seemed a bit overwhelmed to find that Narda's request to "put pictures of fish on the wall" meant not in frames, but instead, in a 25 foot mural in oils.

On the other hand, she thought to herself, it's a stunnin_ expression of talent. "I think it's simply marvelous!" she s_ to Narda. "And I think tomorrow we should visit the art museum, now that I know you have the interest."

"Before I go back to the old routine," Narda thought, "there's one more thing I have to do." And that was...

THE LEAP OF FAITH!
The biggest, tallest, baddest slide at Atlantis.
First you have to climb up a whole bunch of stairs to
the top of the Mayan Temple. Then you sit down at the
top of the slide, take a deep breath and...

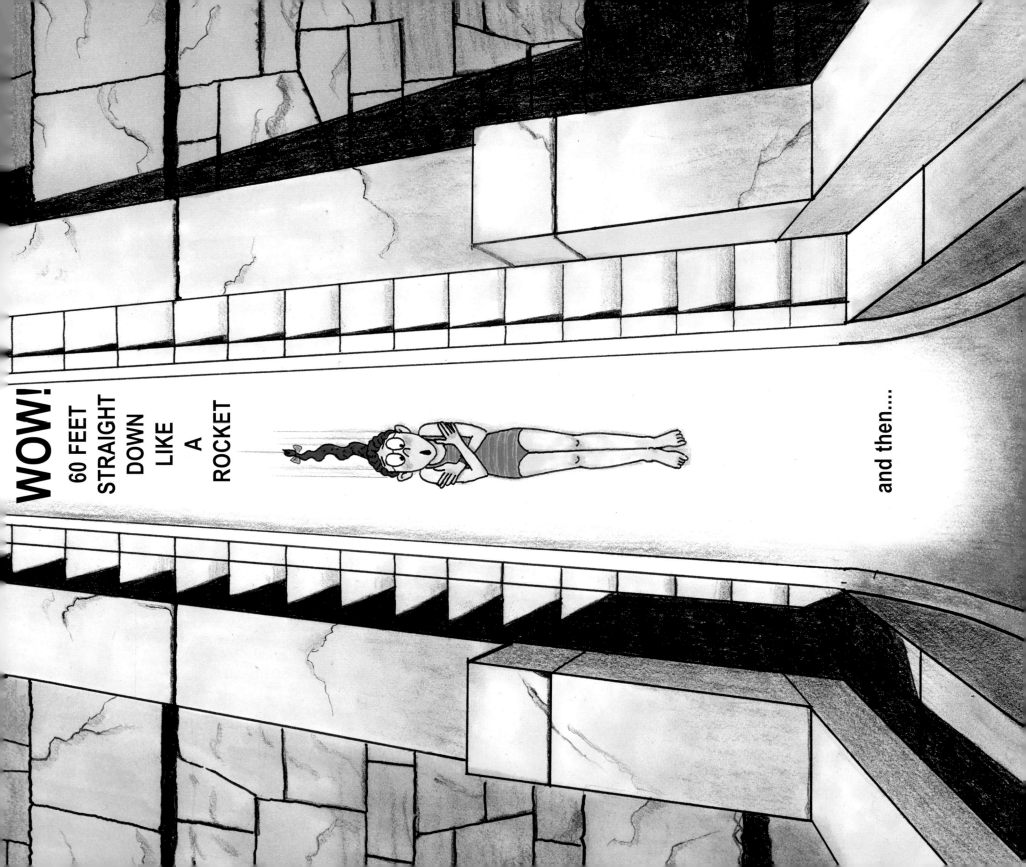

roaring through the shark tank so fast it's all **a big blur**

and then...

shot out into a pool!

Narda LOVED it!

But just as she was climbing out of the pool to go again, she saw a pair of familiar feet. Ms. Colby had obviously recovered.

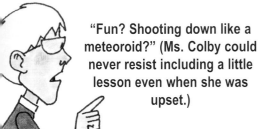

"Narda, how could you possibly do such a scary thing!"

"It's not dangerous, Ms. Colby, it's fun!"

"Fun? Shooting down like a meteoroid?" (Ms. Colby could never resist including a little lesson even when she was upset.)

"Just because other children do it doesn't make it right."

"Lots of kids do it. It's totally safe."

"But that's the fun, Ms. Colby, getting scared a little."

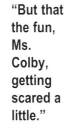

"I don't know what I'm going to tell your father when he comes home."

"Me? On that...that... "

"I think you should try it yourself and then you can tell him what you think."

"Remember what you said, Ms. Colby? The most important thing in life is to keep your mind open to new experiences."

"Well, yes but..."

Ms. Colby, I think you'll end up really enjoying it. We could start on one of the smaller slides."

"I don't know how I let you talk me into this!"

"You'll see. You'll love it!"

SPLOOSH SPLOSH

"Oh, my goodness! I had no idea a mere physical experience could be so stimulating!

"I told you!"

"This time let's go down with our eyes closed!"

OK, Ms. Colby, but let's hurry. They're going to close down soon."

After that Narda and Ms. Colby went snorkeling together

surfing on mats together, and a whole lot more.

"Narda, I have to thank you. I think I'd forgotten what fun was!"

I've had a wonderful time, Ms. Colby. I just wish my dad could have been here with us."

Somebody was listening because Narda's dad came home that weekend!

Daddy!

Narda's dad brought her a necklace from Hong Kong and a silk scarf for Ms. Colby. He kept them all laughing with stories about his trip. Narda was so happy to have him home that she almost shone.

arda," he said, "Ms. Colby told me that when she was in bed you went snorkeling and parasailing and did all the slides by yourself. Is that right?"

"And that you painted a mural on your bedroom wall and you went down the Leap of Faith alone and then talked her into joining you. And she showed me your book on Lost Atlantis about the King not listening."

"Well, yes, but . . ."

"Yes, Daddy . . ."

"Well, it's time for some big changes around here. I can't allow you to do all of these things – by yourselves. So I'm taking off the next three weeks and joining you in the fun. And I plan to be here a lot more often from now on."

"Starting tomorrow! And I've planned a whole day's picnic on the beach."

"Oh, Daddy - You're the best daddy in the whole world!"

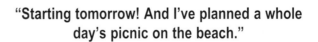

"REALLY? You're going to be home?

The entire next day they spent swimming and sailing and riding
the waves. In the evening they watched the sunset.
For Narda, it was a perfect day.

That night Narda went straight to sleep. And for the first time in a long time .

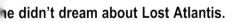
he didn't dream about Lost Atlantis.